Verdi Branch
Washoe County Library

ve WASHOE COUNTY LIBRARY

3 1235 00886 6472

P9-EDF-797

DATE DUE

MAY 1 5 2010			
JUN 1 5 2010			
OCT 0 9 2010			

Demco, Inc. 38-293

Never Babysit the Hippopotamuses!

Text copyright © 1993 by Doug Johnson
Illustrations copyright © 1993 by Abby Carter
All rights reserved, including the right to reproduce
this book or portions thereof in any form.
Published by Henry Holt and Company, Inc.,
115 West 18th Street, New York, New York 10011.
Published simultaneously in Canada by Fitzhenry & Whiteside Ltd.,
91 Granton Drive, Richmond Hill, Ontario L4B 2N5.
First edition

A CIP catalog record for this book is available
from the Library of Congress. LC catalog number 93-18341
ISBN 0-8050-1873-5

Printed in the United States of America
on acid-free paper. ∞

1 3 5 7 9 10 8 6 4 2

3 1235 00886 6472

Never Babysit the Hippopotamuses!

Doug Johnson  illustrated by Abby Carter

WASHOE COUNTY LIBRARY
RENO, NEVADA

Henry Holt and Company • New York

To Peggy, Christopher, Kyle, and Kelsey—
their love and laughter keep me young.
—D. J.

For Doug and Samantha
—A. C.

Never babysit the Hippopotamuses.

To make them forget about their parents,
you'll have to play hide-and-seek....
You should pretend that they are very hard to find.

To let them get to know you, watch a TV show. But don't watch a scary one, or they'll make you look for monsters in the closet...under the beds... in the basement...and even up the chimney.

And be careful if they ask you to dance.
The Hippopotamuses have very big feet.

Don't play leapfrog with them, they can be hard to jump over.

Don't play horsey either.
They always want you to be the horsey.

Oh, never babysit the Hippopotamuses!
They like to play cops and robbers, pirates…

…and lion tamer.

And they love to wrestle….

Sometimes they will even let you win.

They like to play football.
Whatever you do, don't play in the living room.
They are very hard to tackle.

Before you get them ready for bed, you should
make them a snack. But don't make popcorn. They can eat a lot of it.

Oh, never, ever babysit the Hippopotamuses!
Bathtime is crazy.
The Hippos love to do cannonballs into the tub.

It can be quite difficult getting them into their pajamas.

Not to mention their slippers.

And brushing their teeth is not an easy job.

Oh, never, ever babysit the Hippopotamuses!

After you bring them to their room for bed,

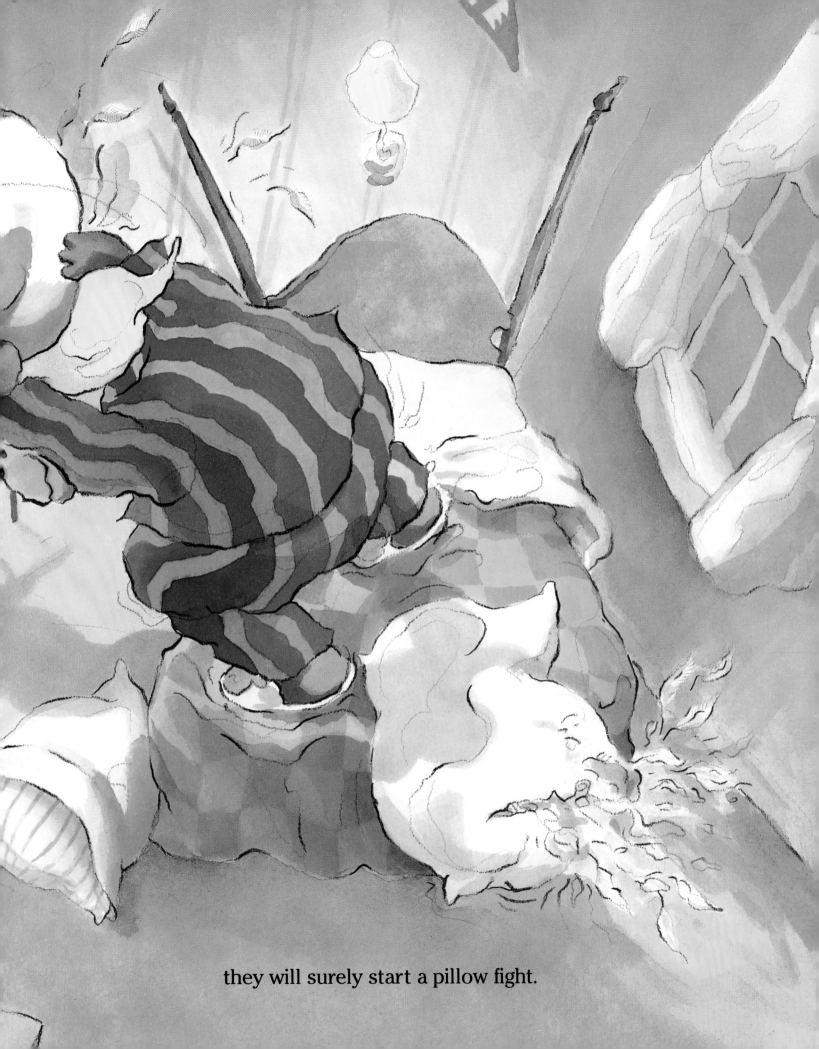

they will surely start a pillow fight.

Then you will have to tuck them in and read them a bedtime story. Remember to turn on the night-light before you leave.

The Hippopotamuses are afraid of the dark,
and if you forget,
they will run out of their bedroom,

and jump into your lap.

By now it will be late, and their parents will be getting home soon.
You must be very firm. Stand on a ladder, look them in the eye, and holler:

"SIMMER DOWN AND GET INTO BED, HIPPOS! NOW!

So. Never babysit the Hippopotamuses.

Unless, of course, your only other
choice is to babysit their neighbors,

WASHOE COUNTY LIBRARY
RENO, NEVADA

the MONKEYS!